To Simon. To Theo.
To all our secret places
well sheltered by majestic trees.
—N.B.-C.

Text copyright © 2023 by Nadine Brun-Cosme

Jacket art and interior illustrations copyright © 2023 by Olivier Tallec

All rights reserved. Published in the United States by Random House Studio,
an imprint of Random House Children's Books, a division of Penguin Random House LLC, New York

Random House Studio with colophon is a registered trademark of Penguin Random House LLC.

Visit us on the Web! rhcbooks.com

Educators and librarians, for a variety of teaching tools, visit us at RHTeachersLibrarians.com

Library of Congress Cataloging-in-Publication Data is available upon request.

ISBN 978-0-593-48698-6 (trade) — ISBN 978-0-593-48699-3 (lib. bdg.) — ISBN 978-0-593-48700-6 (ebook)

The artist used pencil and acrylic paint to create the illustrations for this book.

The text of this book is set in 17-point Bailey Sans Book.

Interior design by Sarah Hokanson

MANUFACTURED IN CHINA

10 9 8 7 6 5 4 3 2 1 First Edition

Rabbit, DUCK, AND BIG BEAR

NADINE BRUN-COSME & OLIVIER TALLEC

RANDOM HOUSE STUDIO ▲ NEW YORK

In the forest live three friends, Rabbit, Duck, and Big Bear. They do everything together.

They play together, eat together, and chop wood together.

They run, hide, and chase each other.

They dance, laugh, and sing together.

They go everywhere together! Everywhere except . . .

. . . they never go down the long, winding path together.

Duck says the path looks a bit narrow for the three of them. Big Bear agrees. Rabbit says it doesn't matter! They already have plenty of other places to go.

Every summer, Rabbit, Duck, and Big Bear throw a party. They prepare everything together. They build things, cut things, and hang things. All through the forest they string garlands with beautiful lanterns that shine until late at night.

But they don't string the garlands down the long, winding path together. For one thing, they are tired.

Plus, points out Big Bear, the garlands aren't long enough. And besides, they should really get some rest before the big party, says Duck.

Rabbit says everything already looks perfect just as it is.

When autumn comes, and the leaves make big golden piles, Rabbit, Duck, and Big Bear play rough-and-tumble games.

They shout and throw big bundles of leaves that explode in the sky.

Then they watch the leaves fall slowly, slowly to the ground.

But they never throw leaves together on the long, winding path.

It wouldn't be a good idea.

It's much too muddy now! says Big Bear.

And, besides, it looks cold down there, adds Duck.

Rabbit asks why even bother, when there are so many leaves everywhere else.

Every winter, when the snow comes, the three friends have a massive snowball fight. They go on long, glorious snowshoe walks together. They ski together. Sometimes they ride down the hill together, all on one sled.

This year is particularly cold. It's so cold that the pond freezes over for the first time ever! The friends get out their skates.

Big Bear is quite a natural skater.
So is Duck, who tries little tricks for the first time. Wow!
But Rabbit has a harder time. So Big Bear shows her what to do, and Duck teaches her how to spin.

The spinning doesn't go well. When Rabbit is back on her feet, the three friends skate together. Slowly at first, and then faster.

As the three friends get close to the long, winding path, Big Bear stops. Duck also stops.

But Rabbit doesn't stop. . . .

She keeps going straight! (She hasn't learned how to stop yet!)
And for the first time, Rabbit finds herself barreling down the path,
not knowing where she is headed.

"Come back!"
"Where are you going?"

But Rabbit is too far away to answer.

Rabbit finally slows to a stop, just before the grandest fir tree she has ever seen. She takes two steps forward, then four. Beneath the enormous white blanket is a secret blue-green world. The wind still blows—but softer, slower.

All Rabbit can think is, *If only my friends were here to see this.*

"Big Bear! Duck!" Rabbit calls.
"Rabbit!" calls Big Bear. "We were so worried!"
"Are you okay?" gasps Duck.

"I am better than okay!" says Rabbit proudly. "Look what I've discovered!"
"Ah, yes, the great fir," says Big Bear. "I love the way its branches cast such long shadows. Especially at dusk."

"Wait a minute," says Rabbit. "You've been here before?"

"Yes," says Big Bear.
"I come here when I
feel like being alone.
I sit very close to the
trunk and breathe in
the pine-scented air."

"But we do everything together," says Rabbit, confused.

"Well, maybe not *everything,* Rabbit," says Duck. "I've been here too. On still mornings I come here and listen to the muffled sounds of the world around me and think."

"*Think?* Think about what?" asks Rabbit.

"Think about, you know, anything."

Rabbit takes in the grand fir towering above her,
then shuts her eyes. She inhales the rich earthy
scent. She listens to the wind's smooth sound as it
passes gently through the needles.

After the skating, her heart is still beating very fast, but she takes a deep breath and exhales slowly. She feels the magic of the great fir. It's almost like her friends aren't even there.

In the forest live three friends, Rabbit, Duck, and Big Bear.

They do *almost* everything together.